MARVEL
SUPER HERO
ADVENTURES

THWIP!
YOU ARE IT!

Written by **Alexandra West**

Illustrated by **Dario Brizuela**

ABDO
Spotlight

MARVEL

Los Angeles
New York

ABDOBOOKS.COM

Reinforced library bound edition published in 2020 by Spotlight, a division of ABDO, PO Box 398166, Minneapolis, Minnesota 55439. Spotlight produces high-quality reinforced library bound editions for schools and libraries. Published by Marvel Press, an imprint of Disney Book Group.

Printed in the United States of America, North Mankato, Minnesota.
092019
012020

© 2019 MARVEL   THIS BOOK CONTAINS RECYCLED MATERIALS

Library of Congress Control Number: 2019942466

Publisher's Cataloging-in-Publication Data

Names: West, Alexandra, author. | Brizuela, Dario, illustrator.
Title: Marvel super hero adventures: thwip! you are it! / by Alexandra West; illustrated by Dario Brizuela.
Other title: thwip! you are it!
Description: Minneapolis, Minnesota : Spotlight, 2020. | Series: World of reading level pre-1
Summary: Spider-Man and friends chase villains throughout the city.
Identifiers: ISBN 9781532143922 (lib. bdg.)
Subjects: LCSH: Spider-Man (Fictitious character)--Juvenile fiction. | Parker, Peter Benjamin (Fictitious character)--Juvenile fiction. | Superheroes--Juvenile fiction. | Adventure stories--Juvenile fiction. | Readers (Primary)--Juvenile fiction. | City and town life--Juvenile fiction.
Classification: DDC [E]--dc23

Spotlight
A Division of ABDO
abdobooks.com

Spider-Man is
a Super Hero.

Spider-Man swings
in the city.
He stops bad guys.
He shoots his webs. *Thwip!*

Spider-Man goes to Central Park.
He sees kids play tag.

Spider-Man loves to
play tag.
He is very good!

Spider-Man sees an
ice-cream truck.
Spider-Man sees Doc Ock.

Oh no!
Doc Ock has all
the ice cream.

Spider-Man has an idea.
Tag can make
his job more fun.

Spider-Man uses his webs.
Thwip! "You are it, Doc Ock!"

Doc Ock is mad.

Doc Ock throws the ice cream.
"You are it, Spider-Man!"

Spider-Man swings away.
He sees kids in the sandbox.

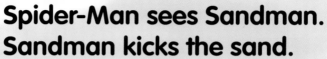

Spider-Man sees Sandman.
Sandman kicks the sand.

Spider-Man uses his webs.
Thwip! "You are it, Sandman!"

Sandman is mad.
He shoots sand.

"*You* are it,
Spider-Man!"

Spider-Man swings away.
He sees people
at the zoo.

Spider-Man sees Rhino.
Rhino lets the
monkey out!

Spider-Man helps the monkey.

The monkey goes back in the cage.

Spider-Man uses
his webs again.
Thwip! "You are it, Rhino!"

"*You* are it, Spider-Man!"

Spider-Man does
not like being it.
Spider-Man has an idea.
He will trick the bad guys.

Spider-Man sees
all the bad guys.
They run away.
They do not want to be it.

Doc Ock goes over the sandbox.

Rhino goes around the sandbox.

Sandman goes into the sandbox.

Spider-Man saves the day!